Rain, Lilies, Luck

Francine Marie Tolf

North Star Press of St. Cloud, Inc.
St. Cloud, Minnesota

Copyright © 2010 Francine Marie Tolf

All rights reserved.

Cover art by Gale Tolf.

ISBN: 978-0-87839-372-5

Printed in the United States of America.

Published by North Star Press of St. Cloud, Inc.
PO Box 451
St. Cloud, MN 56302
www.northstarpress.com

Acknowledgments

These poems appeared in the following publications, sometimes in slightly different form:

Apple Valley Review: "Early Fall"
Comstock Review: "Pascal"
The Externalist: "A Letter, a Request"
GSU Review: "Tragedy Last June"
The Green Hills Literary Lantern: "Elizabeth," "Foster Beach, December," "One Morning at Nineteen," "Snowstorm," "Some Girls," "Strawberry"
Harpur Palate: "Ed, Bragging"
Margie: "That Summer"
Lake Effect: "Tiger Lilies"
Main Channel Voices: "And the Sky," "Summer Poem"
Nanny Fanny: "Lunch Hour"
New Letters: "Boy and Snow Leopard"
Nimrod: "Love Poem for Marc"
Parva Sed Apta: "New Hat"
Plainsongs: "Why I Write About Them," "These Things We Learn," "Typing the Obits"
Poetry East: "Connecting the Stars," "Losing Rumi"
Rattle: "East Rogers Park," "Maybe She Dreams of Rivers," "Snake Blood"
The Rockford Review: "Last Visit"
Southern Humanities Review: "Forty-six," "The Wife of Layman P'ang"
The Spoon River Poetry Review: "Henry Matisse's *Woman Before An Aquarium*"
Umbrella Journal: "Birthday Gift," "For Yehuda Amichai," "Luck," "Sex"

The italicized lines in "Foster Beach, December" are from Lisel Mueller's poem, "Pillar of Salt."
"Pascal" and "Praise of Darkness" appeared in the online blog, *Elegant Thorn Review*.
"For Yehuda Amichai," "Pascal," and "The Wife of Layman P'ang" were reprinted in *ArLiJo Journal*.
"Love Poem for Marc" was reprinted in *Ibbetson Street Press*.
A number of these poems comprised *Blue-flowered Sundress*, a chapbook published by Pudding House Press in 2007.

Table of Contents:

Poet's Market - 1

I

A Letter, a Request - 5
Blue-flowered Sundress - 7
The Wife of Layman P'ang - 8
Talya - 9
For my Sister - 10
Losing Rumi - 11
And the Sky - 12
For Yehuda Amichai - 13
Pascal - 14
Judy Baherling - 15
Tiger Lilies - 16

II

Connecting the Stars - 19
One Morning at Nineteen - 21
Love Poem for Marc - 22
Sex - 24
First Snow - 25
Once in a While - 26
Snake Blood - 28
Strawberry - 29
With Gale, Outside Greenwood Care - 31
Snowstorm - 32
Typing the Obits - 33
Why I Write About Them - 35

III

Henri Matisse's *Woman Before An Aquarium* - 39
That Summer - 40
Lunch Hour - 41
Tragedy Last June - 43
Last Visit - 44
Some Girls - 46
Birthday Gift - 48
Boy and Snow Leopard - 49
East Rogers Park - 50
Maybe She Dreams of Rivers - 53
High Places - 54
New Hat - 55
Elizabeth - 56
Foster Beach, December - 57

IV

Moving to Manhattan, Kansas - 61
Ed, Bragging - 63
Easter at Five - 64
The Last Time I Saw You - 66
Luck - 68
Lone Goose - 70
Forty-six - 72
These Things We Learn - 73
Summer Poem - 75
Hymn, with Birds and Cats - 76
Praise of Darkness - 78
Early Fall - 79

Poet's Market

You gathered everything:
rivers you'd slipped in your pocket,
secrets wrapped in their own roots.
Take these, you urged strangers,
they're all I've got.
All afternoon, people glanced at your gifts,
walked away.
Your heart wanted to shrink to a pebble;
you willed it to remain open.

On the way home, the dark eyes of birch trees
met yours with kindness.
A sparrow nudged into your palm
one small piece of light.

A Letter, A Request

I have been thinking about you, Gauguin,
your final months on an island
where aging cannibals posed for tourists.
I have been thinking about the pornography
you decorated your cottage with,
the twelve-year-olds you bribed into bed;
how despite the oranges and coins, they must have
turned away from your rancid breath,
the oozing, ulcerous leg.
I have imagined the luxuriant penises you carved
on the rosewood cane you walked into town with,
your childish glee at the Catholic priest's concern.

I have shameful dreams of my own, *mon sauvage*.
If I've disliked you, it's not for your sad
debauchery, or the braggadocio you seemed incapable
of abstaining from. It's that thin crack
of hypocrisy that runs through the civilized,
the way you revered your Black Eves
on canvas, then described to a friend your *vahine*,
a girl of fourteen who "got down on her back" for you
whenever you wanted.

I'm a hypocrite too, sometimes
and without the saving grace of genius.
I hope you knew you possessed it,
despite the ridicule in Paris
on your return, your comrades buying paintings
out of pity, and the bad liquor and wormy fruit
you lived on in the Marquesas, cockroaches feasting
on unprotected drawings.

After you died, no one bothered to plunder
the sketches and wood carvings that cluttered
your rooms, the wall panels that bloomed
with winged lizards and flame-colored waves.
They rotted in over-ripe air as your tiny garden
thickened to jungle.

Perhaps I have no talent, you wrote near the end,
for once neither swaggering nor melodramatic,
just a man quietly doubting
his entire life's meaning . . .

You should visit me in a dream soon, Gauguin.
You could tell me whether your fame
amuses you. You'd despise my appetite for guilt,
but I promise you that disappears at night,
when I howl and rage
like any sinner; when I fly like a serpent
through black wind you could paint,
if you bring a brush, with colors you've stolen
from heaven, from hell.

Blue-Flowered Sundress

It comes when I least expect it,
this bitterness towards him.
It brims black from a well
that should long have gone dry.

Eight years ago, in a hospital,
I murmured a prayer over his bloated body.
He looked like a tortoise, my dad,
with his dome of a belly,
his thin, wrinkled neck.
My mother sat lost in the chair behind me.
My oldest sister gabbed on and on.

After the phone call, I paced my apartment,
talking to him out loud. *You did your best,
Dad. I know that. Wherever you are,
believe that I love you.*

But when I shopped for a black skirt
that afternoon, I bought a sundress
instead. And for seconds in shining May air,
as I walked past store windows,
something inside me uncoiled
and hissed to the father who did not apologize,
*See! See what I bought for myself
on the day of your death.*

The Wife of Layman P'ang

In approximately 780, Layman P'ang, a wealthy merchant, experienced Enlightenment. He sold his house and had all of his possessions loaded onto a boat and sank it. He, his wife, and his children then earned a living by selling vegetables and bamboo utensils.

You would not guess
her cheek bones knew powder,
that jasper combs clasped
her thinning hair.

She carries small things
inside her now:
the flower on a baby squash,
an insect's green wings.

When famous men
visit their cottage,
she serves them tea
in clay cups.

They listen with reverence
to her husband
as she enters the room
soundlessly

to kneel for
the used dishes,
the leftover
rice cake.

TALYA

I remember trying not to gag in the front seat
of my first boyfriend's car, sun hard and bright
on the gravel of my parents' driveway,
a boy I did not love whispering
swallow it between moans.

I recall bloodless sex in beige-furnished apartments,
how an attorney wiped his brand new leather couch
with a paper towel to clean the stain of me off.
I walked down twenty flights of stairs that night,
not realizing what a cliche I was, another girl
come to the city, asking strangers to tell her
she was dispensable.

Today in class, a slim branch of a girl
turned in eight lines about waking up
with a boy beside her, feeling only happiness
as she walked four winter blocks to campus.
She has the face of a petal, this girl,
newly-bloomed as her poem, which hurt
the way bird cries at dusk sometimes hurt,
and that sharp, unexpected smell of spring.

For my sister, who wants me to write happy poems

You claim my poems are always sad,
yet I thought without irony today
that the yellow leaves I was walking on
were more star-like than I deserve.
You have a talent for happiness, Katherine,
that I lack – as Elizabeth Kübler-Ross did,
whose essays I am reading.

I'm working on joy, Ross said once
in an interview.
She was then receiving death threats
for helping infants with AIDS.
I can imagine what other gifts
the righteous mailed to this woman
who sensed angels in her living room
and knew joy was a virtue.

I would like to have asked her
what images intruded
on *her* afternoon walks; if like me,
she ever flinched in brightness.

There is nothing we won't do to one another.

But Katherine, I walked on stars today.
I'm working on happy poems.

Losing Rumi

Why couldn't I have left my fresh copy
of *Time* at the airport, or the nubby pink cardigan
I rescued from the waiting area
minutes before take-off?

Why did it have to be Rumi, my Rumi,
with faded lilies on the cover, language
that made me breathe *ah* underlined?
Gone now, pulsing in some bin
full of sunglasses and umbrellas!

I've consoled myself by imagining
a stranger, say a maintenance woman,
sturdily built, thorough,
might sense a humming among lost objects,
plunge her hand into the matrix,
lift out the book.

It could happen. She could read
a passage or two, look behind her, slide
the paperback into her pocket, this thief
who never took so much as a pen
from a motel room.

What choice would she have?
Her entire life, no one's ever said to her,
come, take my hand,
we'll walk into this garden
together.

And the Sky

I felt suddenly like Walt Whitman last night
in the parking lot of Rainbow Foods,
still dazzled from a poetry reading I'd attended,
fresh ponds of rain shining between cars.
I smiled at a boy pushing shopping carts,
he smiled back, it was wonderful!
Inside, I watched a man with dreadlocks
carefully bag the cookies he bought.
I observed four brown-eyed children
unload a paycheck's worth of groceries for their mother.
Listen, I know we're all of us hiding bruises,
but when a veil seems to lift, it doesn't always reveal sorrow.
I saw ordinary people holding doors for each other, saying *please*,
and the sky, when I left, was incredibly lavender.

For Yehuda Amichai:
Letter to a Man Whose Home is Rain

and whose language is the shiver of reeds.
You said of a certain shore that even
God stopped there without
coming any closer to truth.
But it wasn't that wind-eaten beach
or your city of second-hand Jews
("slightly damaged, bargain priced")
that you really meant. *That shore*
is the world,
which you loved anyway,
rubbing its darkness like kindling
between two callused palms until
the flame of a new poem was born.

I love that you were once so jealous
of your ex-lover's lover
you ordered a dog to bite off his penis
(in a poem, that is).
I love that lies were honey to you,
and the purity of anything a myth:
despair *can* comfort,
and hope rip apart our days.

What's a taped-up and pasted-together
product of the Diaspora to do?
Shake a fist at the Messiah you know
isn't coming? Or open your palm
to catch some rain?

PASCAL

Within each of us there is a God shaped emptiness

    Today I saw a blue heron
    ascend from pond water
    with slow, soundless wings.
    It seemed that
    pine trees, clouds of white air
    held their breath
    as two drowsy arcs
    rose and sank
    through pieces of mist.

    I thought: how easy
    to believe in holiness,
    to ache suddenly
    from the loss it carves.

Judy Baherling

Mr. Baherling used a belt on his sons,
but called Judy *Princess*.
He wore a silk vest at her wedding,
his first-born creamy and beautiful.
Who's *your* parents' favorite,
Judy's little sister once asked me,
jabbing a pine needle into her arm.
Like me, she had scabs on her knees,
stormy weather inside.
One chilly spring day, we skipped rope
in my front yard.
Judy chose who could play.
She picked Sherri, then Kathy,
then even her sister. Never me,
ignored on the curb, my fists
tight as hailstones. Decades later,
I remain an unfolded map for any
stranger to read: stunned even now
by that child of eight
who gazed at the fury and love
in my upturned face
with untroubled blue eyes
and a smile that was almost gentle.

Tiger Lilies

Like King David, they have drunk
the wine of astonishment.

Mouths open wide,
they lean toward me in this alley,
swearing the world is good,

that it is easy to live
on fire, unnoticed,
and do nothing but praise.

Connecting the Stars

I knew what would happen when by accident
I met his eyes across the courtyard. I remember his sad
brown suit, the red cloth poppy on his lapel.
It must have been Tuesday, because the Art Institute
was free on Tuesdays. I went every week to visit
a painting of a white horse asleep in twilight,
then sat under yellow trees outside.

I was a secretary at Chicago's most lucrative
law firm. The young partner I worked for
had eyes like dead marbles and screamed *fuck* a lot.
His wife sometimes called, her voice always
teetering on tears.   And here was this stranger
standing over me, fumbling with a sandwich
and a bottle of juice, asking if he could
sit down. He had the sweet, startled gaze
of a boy who wanted me, in second grade,
to be his girlfriend. His hand trembled
when he offered the cheap business card
I later threw away.   I'm not sure why I am
writing about him, or why it's important to include
the painting, and that partner's wife. I can't see
a pattern, but I think of constellations like
Pisces, and Capricorn, which don't at all
resemble their names until lines are drawn
to connect the stars.

It was the first September
since my mother's death. Did I mention the
white horse was impossibly beautiful?
Every Tuesday, I longed to will myself into
that canvas and lie beside him in green dusk,
running my fingers through his untended mane.
There now, I'd whisper to him, *there now.*

One Morning at Nineteen

I close my eyes
and I am there in the dining room
with shadows of branches
patterning walls,
my mother in her pink flannel robe
watering ferns,
my newly married sister
visiting, and me
sketching a plant's jungle-striped leaves
for art class,
happy as I will ever be
and not knowing it,
not knowing
I will keep
the shadows that glide
across my white sketchbook,
the October sun
flooding the hour
with ordinary light.

Love Poem for Marc

I'm no longer surprised when I wake
at 4:30 to darkness.
Sometimes I sink back,
but usually I lie for a time
and think about you sleeping on the couch,
the vodka having finally done its job.

I don't know why last night I switched on the lamp
and began to read an essay about Sarajevo—
parks hacked into tree stumps for firewood,
old women risking snipers for cooking oil.
Hell exists.
But when a witness described
what soldiers did to a mother and son
before shooting them, I put down the book
and covered my face. I had that luxury,
and the luxury of praying,

Which you find absurd.
You'd laugh if I told you I pray for you.
But when you come in the room
after I'm sleeping, and take off my glasses
gently, so I don't wake,
and lift the notebook from my hands,
aren't you doing the same?

I tell you things bother me,
pictures stay in my head,
and you listen, you who will not talk about
the war you were sent to at nineteen.

I think of your body resting heavily,
the dreams you are walking through.
The clouded glass at your side
I will wash and put away tomorrow
while you are still sleeping.

Sex

Who doesn't come to it
damaged in some way? –
needing the other to understand
all that is unsayable?

"Two bodies pleasing each other,"
a writer once described it,
as if one could
slide down experience
into a toddler's playground:

as if its pleasures
came that easily to those
who turn away from cool streams
to reach, with charred hands,
for branches of flame.

First Snow

If I were calmer, I would have listened without anger
to the three men sitting next to me
on the bus. Their boasts about last night's strip club,
their disgust over a dancer's stretch marks
would not have fanned brushfire through blood
that scorched my heart, not theirs.
If I were kinder, I might have noticed
how laughter, sucked dry of song,
scrapes despair.

But it is easy to love this little tree,
barely taller than myself.
They have planted dozens along the path
that leads from the station towards home.
Like a present, it bears a tag naming it "First Snow."
Its trunk is slender enough
for my hand to encircle.

If we are lucky, you and I,
this tree will grow strong,
and gnarled, and beautiful.

Carefully, I lift
a white branch
to my lips.

Once in a While

Forget "the thing with feathers."
Forget that one final gift remaining
in Pandora's box. You know as well as I do
that Hope's a nasty little bitch.
How many times has she teased you into embracing her
only to vanish with an invisible snicker?
And when she recollects herself
a week, a month later,
benevolent, luminous in the distance ahead,
one crook of her finger
makes you forget your pride
and run to her, doesn't it?
She knows her power.
She knows when we swear we are through with her
we don't mean it.

We're not equipped
to resist her temptation.
So we call being at her mercy
virtue, say life isn't worth living
without the grief she gives.
Even if we ignore her, she
sidles into our presence
when we least expect it.
She's the smell of spring rain
in a filthy alley, the red flash of wing
slicing mist; for a moment
worlds open like roses, and it's then
that you better watch it—
she's got you stumbling from
fog into blue air, and light,

and if there's a cliff ahead
you don't care,
the dazzle of her smile is worth it
and sun feels so good
on your pallid skin.

Snake Blood

When I was his secretary, I imagined
the fortune teller – her sign glowing indigo
above the body shop in my neighborhood –
might really work harm.

I wondered if I could do it:
choose the malicious card,
sink pins into waxen flesh,
craft a man's ruin behind moth-eaten curtains
and spit out the guilt.

These days, I don't think of his eyes,
which were dead,
or the neck that grew red with rage
in that penthouse of ice and chrome.
I forgive myself every fantasy in which
he was crushed or demeaned, but

what snake blood can I swallow
to sear the shame of one afternoon
I jumped up from my desk and
brought him what he wanted,
because while chatting on the phone
with his feet on a glass table, he
snapped his fingers at me, twice.

Strawberry

Heart unbruised
by desire.
You trail no blood or violence,
but are sweet to your core, from which
white rays shine
as if the heart of your heart
were an invisible star.

When I bite into you,
my teeth crunch the seeds
other fruits hide.
You wear them gaily, the way
trusting people
wear love on their sleeves.

Foolish little fruit
with your crown of green,
your summer hat that reminds me
of a hula skirt
and tropical islands,
women armed only with flowers
greeting strange ships

With Gale, Outside Greenwood Care

In the last niche of late afternoon light,
my sister and I share a bench outside,
her long fingers cupping
the cappuccino I brought her.

Tom's hanging around, good-natured,
hoping to swap an errand for change.
Alex, tragic, hunches on the bench across from us
staring at Gale with black eyes,
still angry over the cigarette she refused him
two days ago.

Lenny comes up to us offering the sweet smile
of a sixty-year-old smudged little boy,
asking if he can play us a song.

We say yes, we always say yes,
knowing he'll barely suck the first verse of
"Hootchie Cootchie Man"
from his plastic harmonica
before he wanders off,
happy for the dollar I've slipped him.

Gale's fingernails are dirty,
but she's wearing the rose cologne she loves
and the dangling earrings her counselor gave her
for her birthday.

Twelve years ago,
we sat on a different bench
in September's heartbreaking blue,
leaves floating past us,
her green eyes locked so far from light
I wondered if she would ever surface.

Today, thin sun soaks both of us in warmth.
We talk of Lorca, her favorite poet,
laugh over fights we had growing up.
She says she may try to paint again.

Yes,
stones can turn to loaves
in this lifetime.

Her hands are not quite steady,
and her face is deeply lined,
but you would never know from her smile
how brittle she was once,
how she broke, and broke.

Snowstorm

A man's black eyes roll over me,
cool basalt across shoulders, thighs,
slide from my knees
back to a newspaper of sickled alphabet
I do not understand.
I turn again to waves of snow
outside my train window:

Opaque world
where secrets, lashed by wind,
howl unheard truths.

I am immaculate,
untranslated in this whiteness.
My eyes darken,
my whole body softens.

Tonight, I swear,
I will bring home to you this desire,
I will not discard it this time
along the tracks of my day.

Tonight,
I will deliberately finger parted
thoughts for you,
melt boundaries,
speak a perilous tongue.

Typing the Obits

Riley County Historical Museum, Kansas

At first, I did not care
who died, or how, only that their statistics
be fed to the hard drive
before five o' clock on Sunday,
the index cards filed,
my slate clean for the coming week.

As I grew used to my job,
I began to imagine the farmers and homemakers
who had left behind spouses of fifty years:
Veterans and Garden Club Members,
believers in the Resurrection.

"Tess loved to knit doll clothes for her granddaughters,"
one family might offer,
or, "Every Arbor Day, Chuck planted a tree
in his hometown of eighty years."
I'd look at the faces accompanying these words,
see goodness unarguable as a field of wheat.

Sometimes the simplicity of a husband's elegy
("she was my sunshine and my stars,
and I will miss her every morning, every noon, and every night")
made my eyes sting, as did the poems
tucked into a child's obituary,
rhymes about angels and guiding hands
that somehow comforted.

That country of prairie and sky

did not suit me; I longed
for the city I'd left behind,
recalled with a lover's tenderness
now it was no longer mine.

People around me knew what they had;
loved without apology their flat yellow miles
pulsing with crickets,
summer evenings nervous with lightning.

On my last day, Virginia,
whose no-nonsense gaze took stock
of every error I first committed,
gave me a vase of sunflowers
and a note I will keep.

We were moving again.
When you picked me up that afternoon,
unexpected, it was ninety degrees.
Sliding into our old Dodge,
I curved my hand around
the back of your neck,
loving the thick of those muscles.

Too hot for you to walk,
you said. Simple words,
but when I leaned against them,
they held.

Why I Write About Them

I like how the black one sits on our dining room table
with her forearms straight out in front of her, like a sphinx.
I like how the lids of her green eyes
grow heavy when I compliment her,
and how her brother, who is corpulent,
sways from side to side as he walks
with an elephant's slow grace.

Sometimes when he is sleeping in his basket,
warm belly rising like a croissant,
mere purring cannot express his bliss
and he begins to hum.
And the female, who misleads
with her queenly profile,
moans loud with contentment at night—
long, irritating moans, like Keith Jarrett
making love to his piano keys at a jazz concert—
that sink into growls
when she is nudged awake.

I like how their own sneezes
astonish them.
How they lean forward politely
to smell a bare finger,
are lions suddenly when they yawn.
(I like how each yawn ends with an elegant smack –
a slim compact snapped shut.)

They ignore my bad habits.
They endure my wild kisses.
They are not metaphors for anything.

III

Henri Matisse's Woman Before An Aquarium

She gazes through the bowl's curved reflections,
past decorative smudges of goldfish,
focused on something unpaintable.

Decades ago, her bitterness fascinated,
made me feel a little smug.

Strange how I can't find a trace of it today,
studying the contents of her face
in this museum
with its scrubbed white light,
its visitors murmuring like acolytes.

We could be friends now, she and I,
sharing a glass of wine on a blue afternoon.
I could lay my hand on her shoulder.
We could talk about loss.

That Summer

We wore cutoffs and lip gloss that summer,
shy with our new tallness, dreaming of breasts.
We begged for our ears to be pierced, nicked our legs shaving,
walked every evening after supper to the Qwik Mart
for pop and a candy bar, my best friend and I,
thirteen, inseparable,
rippling with dislike towards the girl
who followed us into the store one night
wearing hot pants and platform heels.

She looked about our age,
but her smile was older
as she swaggered past us, soaking in stares
of men buying six packs.
We stared at her, too.
Hated her as she stretched on tiptoe
for a box of Tampax.

Only then, the owner who'd been
looking at her in a way he shouldn't have,
laughed when she tried to pay him.
He said loud enough for us to hear
that he didn't take food stamps.
She was small next to him even in her platforms.
Her voice was a scared little girl's
when she insisted her mom needed this.

We didn't talk about it
as we walked down Raynor Street,
cicadas calling across yards.
We didn't talk about men our dads' age
eyeing her like that,
or how she ran out of the store.
It felt good just to walk.

Lunch Hour

The woman pushing her wheelchair
wears bright lipstick
and coaxes her in a bright voice
to look at the roses
that spill from the iron bars
of the fence they are passing:
coral and fuchsia,
darkest red.

The old woman does not see them.
Thistle-light under her wrap,
she leans forward, puzzled,
as if a sonata were fading
or a loved one had disappeared
into a farther room.

When I walk by,
it is her face I take with me,
not the roses.

Tragedy Last June

In the middle of trimming my hair,
after chatting about her village near Danang
and the blunders she made in beauty school
while English was still perilous,
when I am half dreaming in the chair, lulled
by the hum of the salon's air conditioner,
she stops.
She looks at me in the mirror
with troubled eyes.
"I had tragedy last June," she says.

We had laughed together moments ago,
and the place is empty except for us.
Maybe that's why she tells me
about her son, fourteen last summer,
when he was killed by gangbangers.
Maybe that's why she brings out the portrait
of a handsome and serious boy,
shows me a book in Vietnamese
whose cover pictures a man in long robes
standing against clouds.

"He says body like clothes.
You take clothes off,
the soul still there."

I tell her I believe that. I tell her
I am sure her son is waiting for her,
and her gratitude for my words
shames me, because I do not know
anything, and even as I speak
false comfort, I remember a story by Chekhov
about a carriage driver so lonely
he tries to tell strangers
about the child he lost. I think
how similar our encounter is, I think,
This is good. I can use this.

Last Visit

Not lyrical, the tail-ends
of a life scraped together—
the pumped-up rap
you closed your windows to on summer evenings,
the empty liquor bottles you picked out of bushes
where you watered marigolds once
in green twilight.

Unrelenting, the crumbling plaster, rusted pipes
you shut your eyes to,
leaning hard on memory,
as if the house you had lived in for forty years
were not dying.

Unsparing in detail, my last visit with you
before the hospital—
the stale liter of Coke, the deli salads with expired dates.
The packs of wild flower seeds I'd brought,
both of us pretending, pretending
you would really scatter them
in your small backyard.

Some Girls

Joliet, Illinois

Crazy Kate paces the oval of vapor
cast by a downtown street lamp.
Elizabeth rolls down the car window,
black hair streaming in wind,
calls her a bitch,
throws an empty beer can at the curb.

Joliet, seventeen.
I'm riding with the cool girls tonight,
this town is not yet a dreamwork
of boarded steel mills and lost neighborhoods.
I still swim at the quarry with I-80's cement arcing over it,
still walk after school past the train station
with yellowed marble and broken windows.

I'm one of the cool girls tonight.
Elizabeth's beautiful
in her torn jersey and Levi's.
She tells Kim and Debbie what happened
to a fat girl in gym class,
and both of them laugh.
I chug my beer fast.
If the night's spinning hard enough,
I can stop feeling anything.

Elizabeth runs across blacktop,
chased by the guys who followed us
in their red Trans Am.

I meet her in dreams years later,
kohl-eyed and mocking,
as she walks through my shame.

The downtown is abandoned.
Jefferson Street bridge splits open
above the canal's black water.

Birthday Gift

A poet told me I must
see more than sky
when I look at sky.

But after years
of walking this city's
lakefront,

I noticed only
today, in thin rain,
how perfectly

a white and gray gull
tucked his feet under
each opening wing

as he lifted himself
from rock
to join mist.

I took that gift
exactly as it was,
I carried it home.

BOY AND SNOW LEOPARD, LINCOLN PARK ZOO

His size-eleven Nikes are new.
In nineteen-degree cold
he wears a windbreaker, no gloves.
Hey stupid, he shouts
to the snow leopard pacing
behind bars a rock's throw away.
She ignores him, the only visitor
at her cell this overcast day
before Christmas, sky heavy with snow
that will not fall,
wind off the lake
wire-thin in the stairwells
of project high-rises.
You a ugly motherfucker! he bellows
to the cat, dazzling in her misery,
ebony-patterned fur thick and creamy enough
for the boy's frozen hands
to plunge into.
Instead, they grip a railing
whose iron burns.

East Rogers Park

I dreaded that walk home from the Morse Avenue El stop
to where we lived five blocks away –
the edge of a park by the lake
where even the trees had graffiti
and kids set off cherry bombs nightly
on a beach strewn with plastic caps.

No supermarkets in that neighborhood
we'd moved into for cheaper rent,
only liquor stores with grillwork across grimy glass,
7-11's stocked with overpriced milk and lunchmeat,
a currency exchange with two cameras
and a rib joint that served take-out.

Some people had geraniums in window boxes
they cared for tenderly.
Some people cleaned beer cans and Styrofoam plates
from their yards every morning.
I began to recognize them on my way
to the train, where I stood on the platform
with black girls who tried to act tough,
hawking up and spitting onto the tracks
where the third rail, the one holding death,
stretched innocuously.

Homeless people sometimes slept outside
our first floor dining room window.
I'd go out there on weekends with gloves and a garbage bag
to clean up after the half-eaten food they left,
used condoms and tampons,
urine-soaked clothing.

I tried not to hate that neighborhood, but I did.
I was scared we would never get out,
and sometimes I thought, *why should I,*
why should I be luckier
than anyone else.

Yet with all the chances I took, the alleys
I cut through at night, the blocks
I should never have walked down,
I was never once bothered
as I'd been in better neighborhoods
where I'd had my breasts grabbed, my purse stolen,
a knife thrust at me one evening
by a man in a brown leather jacket
who got twelve dollars, some change, all my IDs.

Never, that is, except once
on Morse Avenue, walking past two black men
spread-eagled against a cop's car
as the officer questioned them and the
usual crowd of gawkers
shuffled and stared.
A Jamaican man with very dark skin and blazing eyes
stepped in front of me, blocking my way.
Why is it always us dey stop
when everyone knows it's de fucking Russians
who run drugs on dis corner,
even someone like you has to know dat!

I wish now I had touched his hand or his shoulder
when I answered him.
I wasn't frightened, I understood
it wasn't me, this white woman he'd never met,
who inspired such rage.
But I simply said, *I don't know, I don't know,
I don't understand.*

And he let me step past him
with an expression that stays with me –
something that might have been beautiful
damaged beyond repair.

Maybe She Dreams of Rivers

I love her because she is exhausted and has fallen asleep on the train
with the book still clutched in one hand
while the other trails the aisle like a willow branch
in slow green water.
   Maybe she dreams of rivers.

Because her shoes are thick-soled sneakers,
and she wears a brown shoelace around her neck
strung with keys that rise and fall in a cluster against her breast
as they ride the rhythm of her sleep.
   Maybe she dreams of horses,
   maybe her body is gleaming and supple.

Because her hair is the orange of cheap dyes,
and her skin is a blend of browns with freckles adorning
a face that is no longer young,
and her earrings are small bells
that are not silver but are delicate
as the eyelashes that flutter now and then,
as if a slight breeze combed the length of our car.
   Maybe June shimmers inside her,
   maybe wind chimes are talking.

I love her because the title of the book in her lap
is *How To Create Poetry*,
and when she awakens with a start,
she looks down at it before she gathers her packages,
pulls a cap over her ears,
   walks out of the train into a wordless winter night.

High Places

He had chemotherapy three times a week,
the senior partner I assisted one summer,
filling in for a woman who'd worked with him
twenty-eight years.

I mixed up files, was slow to learn
software. In air-conditioned cold,
my hands shook with nervousness.

Days when he came in,
he went straight to his office
and shut the door.

Once, in the same afternoon, he gave me back
a letter I typed that had three mistakes,
and learned I had sent an enclosure
to the wrong company.

Frail in his tall chair,
he studied me for a moment
in his sun-filled suite
half a mile above the city.

Intellectual property's a hard line of law
to get the hang of.
I think you're doing just fine.

Four o' clock light
illumined his exhausted face.
I looked away,
my throat burning.

New Hat

Gaunt in stained pajamas, Gale spreads watercolors
across her bed: field after field of calla lilies,
each painting exactly alike.
I told the psychiatrist they were penises.
He's a sadist, he wears a pig crown.

Under the tree stump, where morning glories formed a cave,
we made up adventure stories.
She drew mermaids for me when it rained.

Jade ocean, my sister's eyes. They watch me
this windowless Saturday with eerie triumph.
You're a poet, darling, this place must be hard for you.
What a cute little hat.

It's straw, with a pink rose.
I wore it on the bus, then the train,
then another train, to get here.

I should feel so many things.
All I feel is foolish.

Elizabeth

Once years, once distance,
once a new city
did nothing to dull memories
that tightened my hands into fists.

I don't remember the subsiding,
when cool earth
absorbed the last of my hate.

My hours are rooted now,
my blood feels the pull.

Deeper inside me
than the bed of any dream delta,
words form, dark and moist.

They push to sunlight, Elizabeth,
heal into green.

Foster Beach, December

I'm walking down Sheridan Road,
past high-rise after high-rise,
on my way to Foster Beach;
past candy wrappers and plastic bags that cling
to a chain-linked fence protecting
one small plot of land
where a full-grown elm stands
and beyond it, Lake Michigan,
pale blue and silver
in mid-afternoon light.

I need this sharp air
burning into my lungs.
I need an empty beach covered with snow drifts,
miles of water stretching silently
under winter sky.

* * *

Memory is the only
afterlife I can understand,
and when it's gone, they're gone.
Soon I will betray them.

When I read those words of a poet I love,
I thought, no, she is wrong, I will never betray you.
But I do, of course, a little more every day.
I glance at your picture on the dresser
while reaching for something else.
It's no longer effortless to hear your voice.

* * *

I prayed for your death after that hospital visit
when you didn't know me,
when I helped lift you from pillows
to take one difficult sip of water
and saw for the first time, as your gown fell away,
the body that bore me:
bloated belly, dark bruises,
thin pubic hair.
I covered you and stayed there
until your breathing was almost peaceful.

* * *

I still want to tell you things,
as if you were on the other end of a telephone line,
as if you were really listening.
I can't even dream about you.
Month after month, I dream of a woman with your face
who is not you.

* * *

How you would love what I'm looking at,
here on this bench at Foster Beach,
at the edge of a lake that appears endless.
The water's mother-of-pearl –
now lavender, now pink,
now white as the flakes that drift against rocks.
It's like standing inside of an opal.

That's what I'd tell you if I could,
this hour before sunset: that I closed my eyes
because I couldn't believe such beauty.

When I opened them, iridescence
was everywhere.

IV

Moving to Manhattan, Kansas

We laughed over paintings spread outside of gas stations:
    lavender unicorns, Elvis in mirrored shades,
    lavishly muscled pit bulls baring yellow fangs,
as we laughed over flaming billboards
    warning sinners about Hell; over pawn'n gun shops
    renting silver punch bowls and rifle racks.

It was our way of whistling in the dark, though after all
    people *were* friendly here; we never expected Kansas
    to be like Chicago, our city of fifteen years,
    a mirage now of glass towers and used bookstores,
    sails floating like tents on a misty lake.

But I know you were heartsick as I was
    as we lay on our bed at the Motel 6,
    flipping through old Newsweeks.
It was the article about financial portfolios that did me in,
    made me collapse into tears as you looked up in alarm—
    those pink and gray graphs showing how much in mutual funds
    any competent baby boomer should have earned by now:
    me with $900 in savings, having just quit a perfectly decent job
    to begin graduate school in the middle of prairie
    and expecting you to come with.

I cried as I hadn't in years, told you all I had ever done
    was fuck up. I sobbed over opportunities wasted,
    how my father never loved me,
    how I would die in a state-run nursing home,

And you let me say every word. You opened a bottle of wine
   and poured some for me in a Styrofoam cup, wrapping
   your arm around my shoulder as I sniffled and sipped;
                                               then
you began to do imitations—cowboy, redneck—
   shuffling bow-legged across the carpet
   until I was laughing so hard
   tears started again,

   and started again that night
   when I woke up in a strange motel room
      afraid of how much I loved you,
      afraid of how lucky I was.

Ed, Bragging

Hunched over his computer keys, Ed coughs hard
into his handkerchief, catches his breath, wheezing,
goes on. *I c'n kill just about anything*, he says.
*Ducks, rabbits, squirrels. It don't bother me. Hell,
I shot my own dog once. A Doberman I picked up from the pound.
Come home with some meat from the butcher
and he lunges at me. I says to myself, oh no you don't.
Got my shotgun and nailed that dog right between the eyes.*
He takes a bite of the Danish
he brought for the office.

Ed's son walked away from his three teenaged boys
who live with Ed now in his trailer.
That much I know.
I know that he owned a tavern outside Little Rock,
hasn't talked to his brother in years,
believes all vegetarians are kooks
but calls me "dear" even so.
Also, that he was cut open by oncologists
two months ago and is losing weight fast.

That much I know, and what he told me today,
how his father taught him to be a man one morning
when he was twelve, how he handed Ed a knife
and told him to brace that lamb who'd been following him around
like a pet, brace that animal between his thighs
and slit his throat *like this, he said,
and, Jesus, I couldn't do it. That lamb looked me in the eyes and baaaed
and I couldn't do it. My father beat the crap outta me
in our yard. You're a man now, he said,
you do what you hafta do. After that
I could kill anything.
Din't bother me at all.*

Easter at Five

They must have worked at the dining room table
after we slept—
taken the six baskets from a closet,
assembled the foil-wrapped bunnies, the jellybeans,
the feathery pink and yellow chicks I played with for a week
before losing interest.
I see them clipping price tags from handles,
lining baskets with fake green grass . . .

My father, who loves music, works at the tire factory.
Mom's learning to manage their piano store.
They are sleepy, talking in low tones, laughing a little.
Thirty years later, Dad would ask for the nice nurse
as my mother changed him, cleaning his fingers
with a warm washcloth.

Even then, I could not simply love him.

First up to search for my Easter basket
in the quiet of a dark downstairs,
I felt awe, like in church.
Sweetness filled rooms
from the lilies my father had brought home,
breathing holy and white on the dining room table.

After Mass, we would eat breakfast there,
using the good china.
Mama would arrange the hardboiled eggs my sisters and I colored
on two glass dishes.
Prettiest I ever seen, Daddy would say.
All week, since his daughters didn't like them,
he'd take those sky-blue and lavender eggs
to work, wrapping them carefully in napkins
before packing them in his steel lunchbox.

The last time I saw you,

you were wearing pearls and a mink coat
even I almost admired.
At forty-eight, you never looked better.
Growing up, I was the pretty sister.
You never resented me for it,
nor did I resent, that January afternoon,
your expensive rooms,
the hundred-year-old trees
of that snowy suburb.
Your children were unspoiled,
your husband toned from work-outs
at a private gym. I remember the night the three of us
walked out of a basement bar, singing
"Mustang Sally." Tom lay down on the sidewalk
as you and I pulled him up, more drunk
on laughter than beer.

Not a flicker of that giddy evening
in yours or your husband's eyes
the last time I saw you.
I was careful to refuse wine.
Despite my old parka and salt-stained shoes,
I conducted myself well, I think,
gracious but not gushing,
no slip-ups to regret.

We loved each other once.
My fingers shook when I called you
to tell you I was coming to Chicago.
You were pleasant. Months after my visit,
after five metal stents allowed blood
to again flow from a heart
I dare not examine too closely,
I tore the card you sent me in half,
hating your tiny, neat handwriting,
remembering the brittle courtesy
that stunned
the last time I saw you.

Luck

I used up a life's worth of it in a flash
twenty-five years ago, working as a maid
at the Caribbean Motel on Monterey Bay.
One glittering blue afternoon, without thinking,
I heaved an industrial-sized laundry bag
of wet towels over the rail
of a third-floor balcony.
I'd seen other maids do the same.
It beat dragging the sack down three flights of stairs
after hours of cleaning bathrooms,
then climbing back up.

But the woman carrying her infant across the lot
didn't notice she was in a restricted area.
Twenty pounds of damp laundry missed her
by seconds.
I remember the mother's startled cry,
saw it fluttering towards me
as my knees and stomach liquefied
into something like sickness.

I drank whiskey straight
from the bottle that night.
And because I was twenty-one
and didn't know any better, bought a dozen
sweet rolls at a bakery the next morning
and left the box, along with a shakily written
letter of apology, in the room of the couple
whose baby's skull I had almost crushed.

You'd think I'd be grateful every minute
of my life after that.
But when I ran for the bus yesterday,
reaching the door just as it pulled away,
I wanted to stamp my foot like a child.
I wail to myself about noisy neighbors,
cry over rejected poems. *No luck,*
I think fiercely, sincerely believing
that mantra, as the perilous ice bearing my actions
cracks web-like in ever widening circles,
but continues to hold.

Lone Goose

Every evening, his excited honking
blasts through our dinner as he returns home,
brown wings beating wildly,
feet stuck out in front of him like brakes,
unzipping the pond's smooth surface.

I've watched him on rainy afternoons
swimming in rings, dipping his green neck
into water, then lifting it, cocking his black head to one side,
as if considering the remark
of a goose swimming next to him.

But they're gone now, his relatives
who made a home here last March,
mothers with babies trailing behind them like beads,
adolescents squabbling and nipping one another.
The whole noisy pack flew away one dawn
and left only him,
poking his beak into dandelions,
sitting alone in the sandbox.

When he returns each evening,
he makes a show of boisterous honking
as if an anxious crowd were waiting for him.
That's how proud he is to come back
to a chain-linked pond with a
shopping cart jutting out of the water.

I'm not sure the water's safe.
I worry about kids teasing him.
Why is he so exuberant after flying over miles

of strip malls and shrinking marshes?
He must have something important to say,
because his message reverberates through pine trees
night after night.
It grows more and more human
before evaporating into dusk.

Forty-six

I think of that girl leaning into
a garlic-fragrant evening
from her window above Salvador's Café.

I think of the camisoles folded
carefully in the top drawer of her dresser,
how she splurged an entire tax refund
on shoes.

Would I caution her that black lace nylons
and the lingering gazes of men
do not constitute happiness?

No. She is twenty-four.
Nor would I promise her that life
only gets better, because

that is a lie. I would not even burden her
with a truth: that growing older is
easier than she fears. I think

I would just like to watch her
pull curtains tight, and for animal joy
dance naked in that stucco-walled room,

a bottle of Raven Red nail polish
on the sill by the fire escape,
next to a jar of fresh lilies.

These Things We Learn

I did not know that at seventy-eight,
my mother volunteered to hold AIDS infants
at her hometown hospital.

I did not know her help wasn't needed,
or that twice, that last year of her life,
she failed her driving test.
We were close, but out of pride
she never told me these things,
these things we learn only
after someone we love dies.

It was not until after the funeral,
when I opened a cabinet drawer,
that I found my mother's sketchbook:
crudely drawn little girls, a lopsided picnic table.
I'd forgotten she had once practiced drawing.

Nor have I taken the time to imagine
what late May shadows might have journeyed
across wallpaper as she sat by her dying husband,
ready to close his eyes with her own fingers.

So when I think of what a sister told me,
I think, all right, maybe it's true,
because there are things I will never know.

Maybe when I was young, my mother,
a mother of six, already exhausted
at any day's end, really did take
an abandoned litter of kittens,
helpless and blind, from a corner of our garage,
and cradle the orphans in her palms
before lowering each
into a sink filled with warm water.

Maybe she did this in our kitchen one night,
never guessing a child was witnessing
love's uncelebrated grit, the act
we do not commit but benefit from
when another is willing to bear the guilt.

Summer Poem

I am tired of my dreams' dark interiors
and the family ghosts who inhabit them.
It is July and the man I love has brought home
Bing cherries and watermelon the way my father used to
when I was a child, brown bags of groceries
jostling each other in the back seat of the station wagon,
daughters running out to the driveway
to carry them in with both arms. Downstairs, the rooms
sing, laughter and sun moving easily
from one to the next, a jar of white peonies
on the kitchen sill, a tawny cat
stretched out in glory on the dining room table.

Clink of ice cubes in tea,
hoops of wetness on coasters,
I will bring back these small things,
the freckles on my mother's arm,
how the neighborhood was golden
that hour after supper when the table was cleared
and there was nothing to regret. I will empty
this moldy hurt from my heart until
light fills its chambers, until there is room
for everyone from that house to enter
and know they are welcome.

Hymn, with Birds and Cats

I will praise my failures. I will praise
what I have not accomplished and do not possess
because it has led to this moment
at ten in the morning on a smoky October day,
sitting on the bedroom floor in my bathrobe,
treated to a rectangle of overcast sky
and a poplar whose yellow leaves,
half blown away, are as artfully arranged
as the characters in a haiku.

I will praise my too-small apartment
with its cheap kitchen cabinets
and mismatched furniture, its jumbo litter box
stealing half the front closet whose carpet
is covered with pebbles. I will praise
the dun-colored carpet itself, gayer for wine stains,
and my cardboard box of a desk.
Because I have sat cross-legged there
and felt ideas alight on my shoulder like cardinals.
And my home was a mansion then,
a paradise of the new, which it is for the cats anyway
as they sleep under spider plants
in rich strips of sun.

I will praise my body whose middle-aged belly
protrudes and whose knees have grown knobby,
this foolish animal shape who guilelessly
stared back at me from the full-length mirror
of a doctor's office two days ago.
Because it is still rain- and sun-loving matter,
the same that splashed lake water as a child

and rolled like a colt in June grass.
And I am never more satisfied than when I am
walking or pushing or lifting with it,
loving even the ache that follows,
that assurance I am rooted with earth.

And I will praise my manila folders of failed
and abandoned poems, poems that will never be
published or read by anyone except me.
Because not one was not perfect when first
budding, not one did not leave the fragrance
of possibility between these walls
or deepen what decency I share
with damp soil and oak trees and the geese
honking high above clouds just now,
esteemed messengers I can hear but not see
as I sit drinking coffee, amazed
the ungainliness of my life should coalesce
into something so sleek, so elegant,
as this sudden happiness.

Praise of Darkness

We touch one another
with defter fingers
at night.

Rain sounds different,
its steady falling
a remembered wisdom.

What if the dark waters
waiting to carry us home
slept inside every one of us?

We were loved
before stars existed.
We are older than light.

Early Fall

Faded oranges and rusts, reds rosy and mellowed
as though still faintly warm,
and the many and varied tones of wheat and brown –
today, these muted colors please me more
than the flame of a fiercer afternoon.
And insects are muted too, their modest chirrups and peeps
a soft quilt covering fields on either side of this path.

Our mothers are gone, our fathers too,
but I am not unhappy today, thinking of that,
thinking of how we did not drive to Duluth or Stillwater
as we promised we would in May.
"Spring is the saddest season," my sister Claire claimed,
and I know she is right: every year, that longing
that splits open and sobs –

far gentler, early fall. These wildflowers are enough,
and the way geese journeying south surprise
with the rawness of their calls.
We'll have butternut squash tonight, dusty grapes for dessert.
When I return from my walk,
my old cat will climb into my lap and spread heavy as syrup.
I'll spend time with "The Dead," a story
my students think boring. (Did I think so, too?
For she is walking with me today,
that girl who read *Dubliners* for the first time,
and my mother is close by as well.)

It will be enough, the meal you prepare,
the leaves I collected in a cup on the table.
I'll look into your eyes by lamplight to decide
if they are green or brown.
It will be enough, and more than enough.

Other than my mother, I believe the person I am most indebted to as a poet is an English teacher I had at Joliet Junior College. I will always be grateful to John Stobart – a wonderful teacher – for his considerable kindness and encouragement. I am indebted as well to three poets I met with over the course of four years while living in Chicago: Mark Perlberg (co-founder of the Poetry Center of Chicago), Anne Dirks, and David Pitts. They were my teachers and my friends, and I became a better writer for having known them. Joe Benevento was the first editor to accept a poem of mine for publication (at *Green Hills Literary Lantern*, to my great joy). Over the years, this gifted writer and editor has done me more kindnesses than I can repay. Jonathan Holden and Elizabeth Dodd are two outstanding professors and poets whose workshops at Kansas State University strengthened my craft and broadened my vision. Jonathan, my thesis advisor, went out of his way to support and encourage me. So did my advisor at the University of Minnesota, poet and librettist Michael Dennis Browne. I am deeply thankful for the three years I worked with Michael. Jim Moore and Jude Nutter were my mentors in writing programs sponsored respectively by the Loft Literary Center and by Intermedia Arts in Minneapolis. Memorable teachers both, I continue to benefit from their knowledge and generosity. Marge Barrett and Genie Lerch-Davis are two dear friends who are always willing to read my new work with open minds and generous hearts. I could not have two more supportive sisters than Katherine and Gale. They take joy in my accomplishments as a writer and make the rejections less hurtful. And, finally, there is the man who has driven me to readings two states away; listened to my wailings and insecurities; moved with me from Chicago to Kansas, and from Kansas to Minnesota; the man who knows my weaknesses better than anyone in the world and loves me anyway

Thank you, Marco. And yes, I do love you more than the cats.

About the Author

Francine Marie Tolf lives in Minneapolis. Her poems have appeared in many journals including *Water-Stone, Rattle, Nimrod, Poetry East*, and *Southern Humanities Review*. She has received grants for her poetry from the Minnesota State Arts Board; the Barbara Deming Foundation; and the Elizabeth George Foundation. Tolf is the author of three poetry chapbooks (two from Pudding House Press, one from Plan B) as well as a memoir, *Joliet Girl* (North Star Press of St. Cloud).